Karen's Big City Mystery

Other books by
Ann M. Martin

P.S. Longer Letter Later
(written with Paula Danziger)
Leo the Magnificat
Rachel Parker, Kindergarten Show-off
Eleven Kids, One Summer
Ma and Pa Dracula
Yours Turly, Shirley
Ten Kids, No Pets
With You and Without You
Me and Katie (the Pest)
Stage Fright
Inside Out
Bummer Summer

For older readers:

Missing Since Monday
Just a Summer Romance
Slam Book

THE BABY-SITTERS CLUB series
THE BABY-SITTERS CLUB mysteries
THE KIDS IN MS. COLMAN'S CLASS series
BABY-SITTERS LITTLE SISTER series
(see inside book covers for a complete listing)

Little Sister

Karen's Big City Mystery

Ann M. Martin

Illustrations by Susan Crocca Tang

A
LITTLE APPLE
PAPERBACK

SCHOLASTIC INC.
New York Toronto London Auckland Sydney

The author gratefully acknowledges
Gabrielle Charbonnet
for her help
with this book.

ISBN 0-590-49760-X

12 11 10 9 8 7 6 5 4 3 2   8 9/9 0 1 2 3/0

Printed in the U.S.A.   40
First Scholastic printing, July 1998

What to Take?

Have you ever packed to go somewhere for a whole month? It is not easy. In fact, it is very hard. I was trying to pack to spend the month of July in Chicago with my mommy; my stepfather, Seth Engle; and my little brother, Andrew.

I was sitting on the floor in my room at the big house. Three gigundo suitcases were in front of me. So far one was full of books and toys. One was full of my favorite sheets and towels. One was full of clothes. I was

thinking that maybe I needed one more suit-case.

Knock, knock. My stepsister, Kristy Thomas, poked her head into my room. Kristy is thirteen. I am seven. My name is Karen Brewer. (I will explain about Kristy and the big house and why my mommy lives in Chicago in a little while.)

"Is everything okay in here?" she asked.

"No," I said. I put my chin in my hands.

Kristy came in and sat next to me. "Are you excited about going to Chicago tomorrow morning?" she asked.

I perked up. "Yes!" I said. "I cannot wait to see Mommy and Seth and Andrew again. But I have too much to pack. How will I fit everything into three suitcases?"

"Hmm," said Kristy. "Let's see." She looked in my suitcases. "I do not think you have to take sheets and towels, Karen. I am sure your mother has plenty."

"You think so?" I asked.

"Yes," said Kristy. "And maybe you should take only a few books from your summer reading list. And one or two small toys. Remember, a lot of your stuff is already in Chicago. And Andrew has things you can borrow."

Andrew is four going on five. I had not seen him for two months.

"That is true," I said. I put the sheets and towels back in the linen closet. I put most of the books and toys back where they belonged. I left out three books and my stuffed cat, Moosie, and my stamp set and ink pad.

"Now your clothes," said Kristy. "Remember that your mom has a washing machine and a dryer in Chicago. Take four pairs of shorts, eight tops, three dresses, one dressy dress, and seven pairs of socks and underwear. Wear your jeans and sneakers on the plane. Take a pair of sandals and your dressy shoes. Boom! You are all done."

Kristy is really, really organized. In the end, I fit everything into one big suitcase and my backpack. Now *I* was organized, but I had something else to worry about. What would happen to the rest of my big-house family? I am always such a help to everyone in my big-house family. How would they manage without me?

That night my two best friends, Hannie Papadakis and Nancy Dawes, came to dinner. There are so many of us at the big house that we eat our meals at a long, long table with two long, long benches. Tonight I sat between Nancy and Hannie.

"We will miss you," said Hannie.

"I will miss you too. I will miss everyone," I said. "Who is going to help Nannie with her business?" Nannie is my stepgrandmother.

"I will," said Kristy.

"Who will help Elizabeth set the table?" I asked. Elizabeth is my stepmother.

"I hep!" cried my little sister, Emily Michelle. She is two and a half.

"Hannie and I will take care of each other," said Nancy bravely. "So you can have a good time in Chicago."

"Thank you," I said. Suddenly I felt as if I might cry.

We had a special going-away cake for

dessert. I hugged Hannie and Nancy good-bye and promised to bring back souvenirs from Chicago for them. Then they went home and I got ready for bed.

After breakfast the next morning, I kissed everyone at the big house good-bye.

"Good-bye, Karen!" said Nannie.

"Good-bye, darling," said Elizabeth. "Call us tonight."

"Okay," I said.

I kissed Emily Michelle good-bye. Then I said good-bye to my stepbrothers Sam, Charlie, and David Michael. Sam and Charlie are in high school. David Michael is seven, like me.

Daddy and Kristy drove me to the airport. They waited with me until it was time for my plane to take off. Then we all kissed good-bye a bunch of times. The flight attendant helped me find my seat. And I was on my way to Chicago!

Hello, Little-House
Family!

I like flying. I do not get airsick. I have even flown by myself before. Once I went all the way to Nebraska to see my stepgrandparents at their farm. But wait! I guess you are wondering about all the steppeople I have in my life. I will tell you how that happened.

A long time ago, I did not have a stepfamily. I lived at the big house with Daddy, Mommy, and Andrew. Then Mommy and Daddy got divorced. Andrew and I moved into the little house with Mommy. Daddy stayed at the big house. It is where he grew up.

Mommy got married again, to Seth Engle. Seth is my stepfather. And his parents are the stepgrandparents I visited in Nebraska. Daddy got married again too, to Elizabeth Thomas. Her four kids, Charlie, Sam, David Michael, and Kristy, are my stepbrothers and stepsister. Then Daddy and Elizabeth adopted my little sister, Emily Michelle, from a faraway country called Vietnam. And Elizabeth's mommy, Nannie, came to live at the big house to help take care of everyone, and the pets too. The pets are Shannon, a humongous puppy, and Boo-Boo, Daddy's cranky old cat. Plus I have my pet rat, Emily Junior. Andrew and I both have goldfish. And Andrew has his own hermit crab named Bob.

So now Andrew and I have two families, one at the big house and one at the little house. We have two of lots of things — that is why I sometimes call us Andrew Two-Two and Karen Two-Two. (I got the idea from a book my teacher, Ms. Colman, read to my class. It was called *Jacob Two-Two Meets the Hooded Fang*.) Usually Andrew and I switch houses every month. We stay at the big house for one month, and at the little house for one month. But a few months ago, Seth decided to take a job in Chicago for six months. (He is a carpenter.) So Mommy, Andrew, Seth, and I packed up most of our things and moved to Chicago. (Mommy rented the little house to another family while we are gone.) But I decided I did not like Chicago very much. I missed the big house. I was unhappy, so I came home to the big house.

But now I was on my way to visit my little-house family for a whole month. I could not wait! I missed Mommy and Andrew and Seth soooo much. I missed Seth's cat, Rocky, and his dog, Midgie. I knew I would have a good time in Chicago.

Soon the plane was flying so high that all I could see were clouds below us. We had left the big house a long way back in

Stoneybrook, Connecticut. The flight attendants handed out snacks to everyone. I ate my apple, my cookie, and part of my roll. Then I slept for a little while.

When I woke up, I talked to my neighbor. He had been on a business trip to New York City, and now was going home to Chicago. I know all about New York City, because I have been there several times. So I told him everything I know about it. He was very interested, but then he wanted to nap.

Finally the pilot announced that we were circling O'Hare Airport. I reminded my neighbor to have his seat in the upright and locked position. Then I looked down and saw the runways and little buildings and teeny cars below us.

Tap, tap, screeeech! I sat still until we had come to a complete and final stop. I am a very good flier.

The flight attendant came to get me and let me off the plane first, because I was seven years old and traveling by myself.

Guess who was waiting for me? Mommy and Seth and Andrew!

"Karen! Karen!" cried Andrew. He hugged me hard. "I missed you. I am so glad to see you."

"I am so glad to see you too," I told him.

I hugged Mommy and Seth each about five times.

"Now we are all together," said Mommy. "I am very happy."

"Me too," I said. "We will have a great month."

We got my suitcase from the baggage area and went out to Seth's car. I could not stop smiling. I was with my little-house family again. Hooray!

Little-Apartment Family

In Stoneybrook, my little-house family lives in a little house. In Chicago, they lived in an apartment. The apartment building was six stories tall, with fancy carving on the outside. An awning over the sidewalk protected people from snow or rain.

I had met the doorman, Donald, before. "Welcome back to Chicago, Karen," he said.

"Thank you," I replied.

The apartment was on the fifth floor, so we took the elevator. Everything looked the way I remembered. The floors were made of tile. The walls were covered with patterned green wallpaper. In the hallway I could smell what other people were making for lunch.

Mommy unlocked the apartment door. Seth stood right by the door, and as soon as Mommy opened it, he jumped into the apartment, blocking the door with his feet.

"Back, Rocky!" he said. "Go on, now."

Mommy explained, "Rocky misses being able to go outside to play. He does not like being an apartment cat. So he keeps trying to sneak out the door when we open it."

I giggled. Inside, Seth was holding Rocky in his arms.

"You have to be very careful, Karen," said Andrew. "If Rocky gets out, he could get hurt."

"I will be careful," I said.

Seth carried my suitcase into my room. It was the room Mommy and Seth were using as an office. There was a big desk in one corner, covered with papers. This room did not feel like a bedroom at all. But it was just for a month.

"I have presents for everyone!" I said. "Wait for me in the living room."

I dug my gifts out of my suitcase and brought them to the living room. For Mommy I had a nice box of Nannie's famous homemade chocolates.

"Oh, how wonderful," said Mommy. "Thank you."

"This is for you," I said to Seth. I gave him a picture frame I had made myself. In it was a picture of me holding up a baseball glove that I had caught on a fishing trip.

Seth laughed. "I love it!"

Andrew was squirming on the couch, waiting for his present. I gave him a set of stamps and an ink pad like mine.

"See?" I said. "These stamps are all different animals. You stamp them on the ink pad and then you can decorate notes and papers and books and stuff. I have some too, and we can switch."

"Cool!" said Andrew. "Thanks, Karen."

"I have to get back to work now," said Seth. "But I am very happy you are here, Karen. I will see you tonight at dinner." Seth hugged me and left the apartment. "Get back, please, Rocky," he said as he opened the door.

That afternoon, after a snack, Mommy and Andrew showed me the neighborhood again. I remembered it a little bit from when I had been here before, but a lot of it seemed new. My little-house family had been living here for two months now. People smiled and said hello to them, just the way they do in Stoneybrook.

Mommy and Seth and Andrew had friends here, and a favorite grocery store, and neighbors and everything. But they did not like Chicago better than Stoneybrook, did they?

I asked them at dinner.

"You *are* coming back to Connecticut, aren't you?" I asked as Seth passed me the rice.

"Oh, yes, honey, definitely," said Mommy.

16

"Seth will have work here for several more months. But then we will pack up and come home. I promise."

"Okay," I said. I started eating my chicken.

"Now, let's see," said Mommy. "Andrew has summer preschool every day until one o'clock. Seth goes to work around eight-thirty. And I've been learning how to make jewelry in the mornings. A friend of mine is teaching me."

"When I come home from preschool, we can do lots of fun stuff," said Andrew. "Mommy and I want to take you to the zoo and the children's museum and any other place you want."

I smiled at him. "I cannot wait."

That night I slept in "my" bed, with the noises of Chicago down below me in the street. It was nice to hear Mommy's voice in the other room.

Life in Chicago

The next morning Seth left for work before I even finished breakfast. Then Mommy and I walked Andrew to his preschool two blocks away. On the way home, Mommy and I stopped at a fruit stand and bought some bananas and some nectarines.

In Stoneybrook, we usually drive everywhere. Here, it was easier to walk.

Back at the apartment, Rocky *almost* made it out the door when we opened it. But I blocked him with my feet. "No, no, Rocky," I said. "We do not want you to get lost."

I helped Mommy make the beds and load the breakfast dishes into the dishwasher. Then I picked up Andrew's and my toys and put them neatly in our rooms.

Mommy hugged me. "I have really missed having my special helper," she said.

For awhile Mommy and I sat together on the couch, talking. Although we talk every day on the phone when I am in Stoneybrook, it is not the same. I was so happy talking to her face-to-face. I told her what I had been doing all summer. She told me how she had been learning to make beautiful jewelry out of silver and pewter (which is like silver, only not as shiny). Mommy told me about the art projects Andrew had been doing at preschool, and about Seth's work. Seth had been working very hard here.

"We are looking forward to moving back," said Mommy.

I was glad to hear it.

Soon Mommy decided to practice making her jewelry. She showed me her tools — tiny pliers and tiny clamps and even wax, to practice designs on. "I cannot melt silver or pewter here in the apartment," she said. "I do not have some of the equipment. And it would be a fire hazard. So I have to go to my friend's studio for that. But I can do other things."

Mommy needed peace and quiet to work, so I wandered around the apartment, looking for something to do. At the big house, I could have watched TV or played with my Moonbeam video game system. But Mommy and Seth do not approve of watching too much television. And I did not have my video game system with me.

For awhile I sat on the radiator cover in the living room and looked out the window at the street below. From five stories high I could see up and down the block. I could see people on bicycles making deliveries from the grocery store and the pharmacy. I saw many people walking dogs.

Soon I realized something: I was bored, bored, bored. I wished I could ask Mommy to think of something for me to do, but I did not want to disturb her. I wanted to show her that I could be a big girl and entertain myself. But it was not easy.

I wandered around the apartment some more. Andrew had gotten a few new books and games, and I read them and played with them. But books for a four-going-on-five-year-old are not what a seven-going-on-eight-year-old wants to read. And I could not play the games by myself.

Rocky was napping. Midgie was napping. *That* had not changed, I thought. I lay on the couch, looking up at the ceiling. I tried to read one of my books. This is not good, I thought. It is my second day here and I am already bored.

I decided to work on drawing. Andrew was doing all sorts of art projects at pre-school. Mommy was making jewelry. Seth made beautiful furniture. I should do something artistic too.

That is what I did until lunchtime. I drew. I drew Rocky and Midgie. I drew Mommy's spider plant. I drew Andrew's bed with his stuffed animals on it. I drew things I saw out the living room window.

Finally it was lunchtime. Mommy and I ate turkey-and-cheese sandwiches with potato chips. Then we put Midgie's leash on her and walked her to the small park around the corner. At last it was time to pick up Andrew — hooray! Mommy and Midgie and I walked to his preschool. I went into Andrew's classroom. I was very glad to see him.

Once we got home, it was much more fun. Andrew and I played board games. We played word games. We told each other stupid jokes. I was having a good time in Chicago.

Laundry in the Basement

By the end of the week I almost felt as if I belonged in Chicago. This visit was very different from my last visit. This time I already knew I would be going back to Stoneybrook at the end of the month, so I was not worried or unhappy. It was easy for me to feel comfortable in Chicago.

Every day was the same and also different. In the mornings, after Seth went to work and Andrew went to preschool, I helped Mommy around the apartment. I do not know how she had managed without me. I was helpful in so many ways.

First we tidied up the apartment together. Then Mommy practiced her jewelry making. After a few days, Mommy let me take Midgie for her morning walk *all by myself.* I could only go up and down our block, where Mommy could see me from our windows. Of course, I could do this in Stoneybrook. But Chicago is a big city.

Sometimes I helped Mommy with the laundry. Back in Stoneybrook, our washer and dryer are in the basement of our house. Here, the washers and dryers were in the basement of the apartment building. Mommy went with me the first couple of times to show me where everything was.

This is how we did our laundry: First we put it in a little cart with wheels. (We also used the cart for groceries.) Then we rolled the cart down the hall to the elevator. We pushed the button that said B, for basement. The basement was gigundo. It had bright white walls and gray tile floors and signs on the walls. One sign said EXERCISE ROOM. One sign said SUPERINTENDENT. The superintendent is the person who takes care of the apartment building. (Sometimes he is just called the super.) Another sign said LAUNDRY ROOM.

We followed the signs to the laundry room. Along the halls were other doors, which were locked. They were just for the super.

Inside the laundry room were more washing machines and dryers than I had ever seen in one place. The washers were in two rows in the middle of the room. The dryers were around the walls of the room. The dryers were so huge that I bet Hannie and Nancy and I could all fit inside one of them!

There was also a change machine and a soda machine, long tables to fold laundry on, and a small round table with chairs, in case you wanted to sit and wait for your clothes to wash. Everything smelled like detergent and dryer sheets and fabric softener and warm clothes.

I loved the laundry room.

Mommy sorted the laundry and put four loads into four different machines all at the same time. "They should be done in about half an hour," she said, looking at her watch. "Then we will put them into two dryers. This is where we put the quarters." She showed me the money slots.

"I get it," I said, nodding. "I can do it."

"Okay," said Mommy, and we went back to our apartment.

After half an hour, I left our apartment. "Back, Rocky," I said, shooing him away with my foot. I went down the hall to the elevator and pressed the B button. I felt so, so important. I bet people were surprised to see that I was old enough to do laundry all by myself.

In the basement I walked straight to the laundry room. Other people were there, folding clothes or taking clothes out of the dryers. I opened our washers, pulled out the wet clothes, and put them into two dryers. Then I dug some quarters out of my pocket

and put them into the money slots. I pressed a button. Like magic, the wet clothes started flopping around in a big circle.

I turned and went back upstairs. Another job well done.

Rocky Escapes!

Over the next week, I explored the rest of the apartment building. I could go all over it, as long as I stayed inside and did not go into any apartments.

All of the floors looked pretty much the same. Everyone's front door was painted black. On every floor was a trash chute where you could throw your trash down to the basement. Sometimes people put interesting things, such as old lamps or broken chairs, by the trash chute. (Back in Stoneybrook, we just put our trash in a plastic can and set the can by the street. Borrrring.)

Sometimes I could hear people talking inside their apartments, but I did not stay to listen. That is not polite. Mostly I stayed in the lobby. The lobby was a very interesting place. People were always coming and going. Donald, the doorman, opened the door for them, and he also took packages from the Fed Ex man and another deliveryman, whose name was Fred. Sometimes I saw the mail carrier come to deliver all the mail. With one key, she opened a whole wall of mailboxes! Then she sorted the mail into the boxes inside and locked the wall up again. I started to think that maybe I would like to be a mail carrier in a big city someday.

I also liked to watch people taking their dogs on walks. Midgie knew a lot of these dogs. She had her own dog friends in our building. After a while, I got to know them too.

Then, on Thursday, it happened. Mommy went downstairs to see if a jewelry-making catalog had arrived in the mail. When she came back into the apartment, Rocky shot out between her feet!

"Karen! Help!" cried Mommy.

I dashed to the front door in time to see Rocky fling himself around a corner and race upstairs to the sixth floor.

"I will get him!" I shouted, and pounded after him.

Well. If you have never chased a galloping cat, you might not know that they are very, very, very fast. Rocky was running down the sixth-floor hall before I even made it to the top of the steps. I chased after him.

When he reached the end of the hall, he realized he was trapped — almost. Before I knew what he was planning, he turned and ran right past me, toward the stairs again! I leaped for him, but he flashed past too quickly.

"No, Rocky!" I called. "Come back here!"

But he was already padding silently down the stairs.

I grabbed the banister and raced after him. One flight of stairs, two flights. I ran as fast as I could, but Rocky was always faster. Then I had a bad thought: What if he made it to the lobby, and the front door was open? He might run out in the street! He might get hit by a car.

"Catch that cat!" I yelled at the top of my lungs. "Do not let that cat escape!"

In the lobby, Donald saw me run down the last stairs. "He went that-a-way," he said, pointing toward the mail area.

I slowed down. I could hardly breathe. Very, very quietly, I snuck over to the little alcove with the mailboxes. I peeped around the corner. There, looking scared, was Rocky.

I got down on my hands and knees and crawled very slowly and calmly around the corner. "Hi, Rocky," I said softly. I tried to act casual, as though I found him in the lobby every day of my life.

"Hey, boy. What are you doing down here?"

Rocky began to look less scared. I crept toward him, holding my breath.

"Come on, now," I said. "Mommy is waiting for us upstairs. It is almost time for lunch. Okay? Can I pick you up?"

Rocky did not move. He seemed almost glad to see me. I do not think he had ever been in the lobby before.

I put my hands around his tummy and gently picked him up. I cradled him against my shoulder and supported his feet.

"Good boy," I said, slowly standing up.

Donald smiled and gave me the thumbs-up sign as I walked to the elevator, holding Rocky. Rocky had calmed down and was washing one paw over my shoulder.

Two other people were in the elevator. "Five, please," I said politely. A man pushed the button for me.

I got off at five and began to walk to our apartment. Suddenly an alarm sounded! Rocky almost leaped from my arms again, but I held him very tightly. There was a loud clanging in our ears. Ahead of us, Mommy opened the front door, looking worried.

"Mommy, Mommy!" I said. "Is it a fire?"

Not a Fire

"I do not know, Karen," said Mommy. "Please come inside and I will call Donald."

Donald always knew what was going on.

Mommy picked up the small phone by the front door and spoke into it. "Yes," she said. "I understand. Thank you."

Mommy turned back to me. (I had let Rocky go. He was eating a snack by the kitchen sink.) "It is not a fire," she said. "It is a burglar alarm. There has been a robbery in the building."

I gasped. "You are kidding! Where?"

"I am not sure," said Mommy. "But the police are on their way."

I headed for the front door. "I have to go ask Donald what happened," I said.

"Wait, please, Karen," said Mommy. "I would like you to stay in our apartment while the police are trying to do their job. We do not know where the burglar is or what happened." She hurried to double-lock our door. A shiver went down my spine.

Since I could not go out, I ran to the living room window and looked down. It was not long before two police cars drove up and parked quickly. Three policemen and one policewoman got out of the cars and raced into our building. I was dying to go down to the lobby, but I knew Mommy was right. We should stay safely inside.

Once the police were in our building, I could not see them anymore. I listened carefully, but I could not hear anything. No yelling or running. I felt sorry for Andrew, who was at preschool. He would be upset

36

that he had missed all the excitement. Then I remembered my little camera. At least I could take pictures for Andrew. I got it from my room, then opened the living room window. (There are safety bars on it so I could not fall out.) I put my camera through the bars and took pictures of the police cars below.

For almost an hour nothing happened. I did not move from my spot. Rocky sat next to me. I think he was trying to apologize for making me chase all over the building after him. Then I gasped again. I had been *all over* the building that morning, chasing Rocky! Maybe I had seen the burglar!

I thought and thought, but could not remember a single suspicious person. No one had been dressed all in black, holding a tool bag and carrying a flashlight. No one had been wearing a black mask. I was disappointed. If I had seen someone, I could have been the star witness for the police. I would have been famous.

Finally the police cars drove away, and

Mommy said I could ask Donald what had happened. I shot out the door so fast that Rocky never even had a chance to follow me. I raced down the five flights of stairs. (The elevator would have taken too long.) Several other people were in the lobby, crowded around Donald. I wormed my way to the front.

"Donald! Donald!" I said. "What happened?"

Donald looked concerned. "Nothing like this has ever happened in this building before," he said. "But apartment number forty-seven was broken into this morning. Several valuable paintings were taken."

An older woman said, "Oh, no!"

"No one was hurt," said Donald quickly. "The apartment was empty at the time. And the police have determined that the thief is not hiding anywhere in the building. We are perfectly safe."

"But how did someone get in?" asked Mr. Beakins. (He lives on the sixth floor.)

"We are not sure," said Donald. "I was on

duty all morning, and did not see anyone suspicious. The basement doors and windows are locked and barred. Even the door to the roof is locked. It is a mystery. But I am sure the police will solve it soon."

I wandered back toward the elevator, my head buzzing with ideas. A robbery! Right here in our building!

The Mystery

Apartment forty-seven was on the floor below ours. I decided Mommy would probably not mind if I just *looked* at its door. That would not be dangerous. So I got off the elevator on the fourth floor.

Right away I could spot apartment forty-seven. The policewoman was still standing in the doorway, making notes for her report.

"Excuse me," I said politely to her. "I do not mean to bother you. But have you cracked the case yet?" ("Cracked the case" is

what detectives say. It means "solved the crime.")

The police officer looked at me and smiled. "No, I am afraid not. We are still gathering information."

"What kind of information?" I asked eagerly. I am probably the most curious person I know. Not knowing things makes me crazy.

"I am sorry, but our report is confidential," the officer said kindly. "Unless you have anything you would like to add to our report. Did you see or hear anything?"

I was dying to be able to say, "Yes! I saw the whole thing!" But I could not. That would be fibbing. Fibbing to a police officer is very, very bad.

I had to shake my head. "No," I admitted sadly. "I did not see a thing. Even though I was chasing my cat all over the building."

"Oh, too bad," said the officer. She finished writing her report, then spoke into her walkie-talkie. "Good-bye," she said to me.

"Good-bye," I said.

I watched her get into the elevator. Then I looked at the front door of apartment forty-seven. It was closed. There was gray dust on it because the police had dusted for finger-prints.

Suddenly I felt someone watching me. A shiver went up my spine. Slowly I turned. What if the burglar had come back?

"Do you need something?" asked a boy.

He looked like he might be my age. He had dark brown hair cut short above his ears. He had brown eyes.

I was very relieved. He could not be the burglar. Then I remembered the first rule about solving a mystery: *Everyone is a suspect.*

"Nothing *you* could help me with," I said. I crossed my arms over my chest. "What are you doing here, anyway?"

"I live here," he said.

"In number forty-seven?"

"Yes. It is my grandmother's apartment. My mother and I are visiting her for a month."

I felt a tingle of excitement. This boy could be an important source of information!

"Were you here when the apartment was broken into?" I asked. "Do you, your mother, and your grandmother have alibis? And what is your name? You do not have a criminal record, do you?"

"My name is Matt Dilley," he said. "Of course I do not have a criminal record! And my mother and grandmother and I were all out doing errands this morning. Not that it is any of your business."

"It is my business because I live in this building," I said. "Was anything besides the paintings stolen?"

Matt rolled his eyes. "Nothing. Just the dumb old paintings."

"Are there any suspects?" I asked.

Matt rolled his eyes again. He was being a pain. "No, of course not. The police just started working on this case."

My eyes narrowed. Mr. Smarty-pants Matt might think it was none of my business, but I knew better. I knew this was a case for Detective Karen Brewer. I would be in Chicago for another two and a half weeks. I knew I could solve the mystery by then.

"Excuse me. I have to go now," I said.

"What is your name, anyway?" asked Matt.

"Karen Brewer," I said. "I live in apartment fifty-one. Just for this month."

Then I turned and walked up the stairs. I could feel Matt watching me leave.

MY PROGRESS

OFFICIAL ROBBERY NOTEBOOK
OFFICIAL ROBBERY NOTES
BY DETECTIVE KAREN BREWER

FRIDAY, 9:47 IN THE MORNING
THIS MORNING I TALKED TO DONALD THE DOOR-
MAN AGAIN. HE SAID HE HAD NOT SEEN ANYONE
SUSPICIOUS LEAVING THE BUILDING WITH BIG
PACKAGES. "NO ONE IN A BLACK MASK?" I
ASKED. "NO," HE SAID. QUESTION: HOW DID
THE BURGLAR ESCAPE, CARRYING SEVERAL LARGE
PAINTINGS?

MONDAY, 11:05 IN THE MORNING
SOON MOMMY WILL WANT ME HOME FOR LUNCH.
I AM IN THE LOBBY, HIDING BEHIND THE BIG
PALM PLANT IN THE CORNER BY THE ELEVATOR. I
CAN SEE EVERYONE COMING AND GOING. SO FAR,
NO ONE HAS SAID ANYTHING SUSPICIOUS, SUCH AS
"I WONDER HOW I WILL SELL THOSE PAINTINGS I
STOLE." BUT I AM STILL WATCHING.

TUESDAY, 2:30 IN THE AFTERNOON
I AM WAITING FOR MOMMY AND ANDREW TO
COME DOWNSTAIRS. WE ARE ALL GOING TO A
MUSEUM. I HAVE MY CAMERA WITH ME. I
HAVE BEEN TAKING PICTURES OF SUSPECTS.

SUSPECT LIST
1) EVERYONE IN THE BUILDING (EXCEPT ME,
MOMMY, SETH, AND ANDREW.)
2) DONALD? (HE SEEMS INNOCENT.)

SO FAR I HAVE GOTTEN PICTURES OF MR. BEAKINS
AND MRS. BORGEN AND DONALD, PLUS FIVE
OTHER PEOPLE IN THE BUILDING. I WILL HAVE THE
PICTURES DEVELOPED AS SOON AS I TAKE THE LAST

TWO PHOTOS ON THE ROLL OF FILM.

WEDNESDAY, 10:30 IN THE MORNING
BURGLARY FACTS
1) NO ONE SAW ANYTHING.
2) NO ONE HEARD ANYTHING.
3) APARTMENT FORTY-SEVEN WAS BROKEN INTO.
QUESTION: WERE MATT, HIS MOTHER, AND HIS
GRANDMOTHER REALLY OUT DOING ERRANDS?
HAVE THE POLICE CHECKED THIS?
4) THERE IS NO WAY IN OR OUT OF THE BUILDING
WITHOUT GOING PAST DONALD. QUESTION: DID
THE BURGLAR USE GIANT SUCKER CUPS ON HIS
HANDS AND FEET AND SUCKER HIS WAY DOWN
THE OUTSIDE OF THE BUILDING? (I SAW A MOVIE
LIKE THAT ONCE.)
5) PAINTINGS ARE BIG. HOW DID THE THIEF HIDE
THEM WHEN HE (OR SHE) LEFT?

SATURDAY, 7:30 AT NIGHT
I DID NOT DO MUCH TODAY ON THE CASE.
MOMMY, SETH, ANDREW, AND I WENT TO PICK
STRAWBERRIES IN WISCONSIN. IT WAS A LONG

48

DRIVE, BUT PRETTY. AND NOW WE HAVE SEVEN-
TEEN POUNDS OF DELICIOUS STRAWBERRIES! YUM.
I AM EXHAUSTED. I AM GOING TO BED.

SUNDAY, 8:00 AT NIGHT
I AM IN BED. I DID NOT DO MUCH ON THE CASE
TODAY. THERE WAS A KITE-FLYING FESTIVAL IN THE
PARK AND WE ALL WENT. SETH HELPED ANDREW
AND ME FLY OUR KITES. WE GOT THEM UP
REALLY HIGH! THEN WE HAD ICE CREAM
BEFORE LUNCH. NOW MOMMY SAYS I MUST
TURN OUT THE LIGHT. I WILL BE BACK
ON THE CASE TOMORROW, AS SOON AS ANDREW
GOES TO PRESCHOOL.

MONDAY, 2:00 IN THE AFTERNOON
I WAS DISCUSSING THE CASE WITH MY JUNIOR
DEPUTY, ANDREW BREWER. THEN SUDDENLY
I REALIZED: IF THERE IS NO WAY THE BURGLAR
WAS ABLE TO SNEAK THE PAINTINGS OUT OF
THE BUILDING, MAYBE THEY ARE STILL
HERE SOMEWHERE. HIDDEN SOMEWHERE IN
THE BUILDING! ANDREW ASKED IF THEY COULD BE
FOLDED UP SMALL. I SAID I DID NOT THINK SO.

SO NOW I AM GOING TO SEARCH THE BUILDING FROM TOP TO BOTTOM. ANDREW SAYS HE WILL HELP ME, WHEN HE IS NOT AT PRESCHOOL. AT LAST! WE ARE ON THE RIGHT TRACK.

Rocky's Second Great Escape

I finally took the last two pictures on my roll of film. (One picture was of Midgie and Rocky snuggled up together on the living room rug. The other was of Andrew toasting me with chocolate milk.)

Mommy and I took the pictures to the drugstore to get them developed. It would take two whole days. I was very disappointed. Two days is a gigundoly long time when you are on a case.

In the meantime, I kept up with my notes. I managed to interview the Petersons, who live next door to apartment forty-seven. They had not heard or seen anything out of the ordinary on the day of the burglary. I was getting a little discouraged, to tell you the truth. I have solved mysteries before. But it has never taken so long to get one measly clue.

It was time to search the building for the missing paintings. Starting on the top floor and working my way down was the best plan. I climbed the staircase to the sixth floor. There was the door that led to the rooftop, but I was not allowed to open it. Mommy had said I must never, ever go out onto the roof without her. Sometimes it is hard being a seven-year-old detective. If I were a grown-up detective, I could go out on the roof with no problem. If the paintings were up there, I was out of luck.

Anyway, I searched every inch of the sixth-floor hallway. There was not even one single solitary place that someone could have hidden a painting. I even looked by the trash chute and behind the table by the elevator. Nothing.

My plan was to keep searching after lunch. And when Andrew came home, he could help me. Or at least keep me company while I looked. But it did not work out that way.

I returned to our apartment, my head hanging low. My notebook and pen were tucked into the waistband of my shorts. I guess I was not really paying attention when I took my door key from its chain around my neck and unlocked our apartment.

"Karen, watch out!" called Mommy.

I jumped back, but it was too late. Rocky shot out the door between my feet and raced down the hall. "I will get him!" I yelled. Then I dropped my notebook and pen by the door and tore after our cat.

I think Rocky had learned his way around the building the last time he escaped. Because he headed right for the elevator doors. And this time they were open!

"Do not let that cat in the elevator!" I cried. "He is not allowed!" But Rocky managed to leap inside just as the doors swished shut. I skidded to the elevator, only to see the closed doors staring me in the face. Quickly I looked at the lighted numbers above the doors. The elevator was heading down.

"Oh, please, not the lobby again," I muttered. I turned and started pounding down the steps. On each floor I poked my head around the corner to see if the elevator had stopped there. It had not. It did not even stop at the lobby. Rocky was headed for the basement!

I yanked open the basement door and ran down the steps. I got there just as Rocky sauntered out of the elevator behind Mr. Rajid, who was carrying a duffel bag of laundry.

"Rocky!" I called. "Come here, boy!"

That naughty cat. As soon as he heard my

voice, he tucked his tail between his legs and started galloping toward the laundry room. I sighed and ran after him.

Well. There were a million places for a cat to hide in that basement. Finally, after about half an hour, I saw Rocky disappear into a dark doorway, where the janitors kept extra mops and brooms. I ran after him and flicked on the light.

The first thing I saw was a pair of scuffed red sneakers with holes over the pinkie toes.

Rocky was winding his way around a pair of jean-covered legs. Slowly I looked up, and saw . . . Matt Dilley! My eyes narrowed. He was wearing a small tan trenchcoat and sunglasses. And here he was hiding in a dark room. Talk about suspicious behavior.

"You!" I said. "What are you doing here?"

"Nothing," said Matt, trying to look casual. "Just hanging out."

"In a broom closet? In the basement? In the dark?"

Matt shrugged. "What are *you* doing here?" he asked.

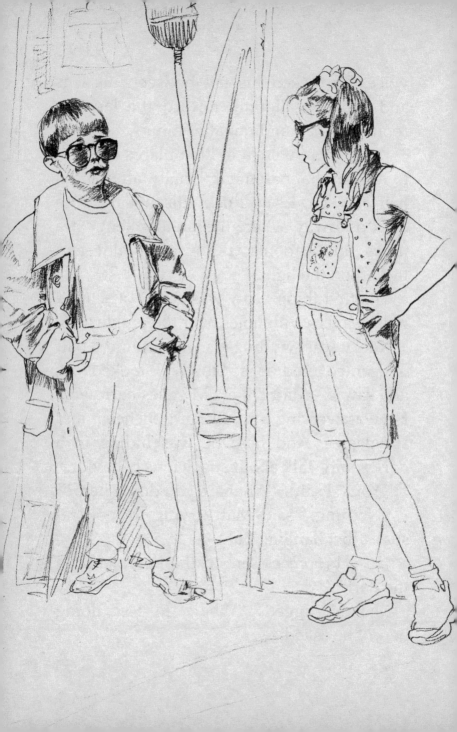

"Getting my cat." I leaned over and scooped up Rocky, who seemed worn-out from all the running.

"Suuuure," said Matt, sounding just as suspicious as I.

"Well, here he is!" I said, holding Rocky up. "Do you think I am making it up?"

Matt looked unconvinced. "Maybe you and the cat are working together."

I stared at Matt. I could not think of anything to say, so I turned around and carried Rocky to the elevator. He was purring.

I frowned fiercely at Rocky, but he did not seem to mind.

Matt the Suspect

"Andrew, Andrew, the pictures are here!" I said on Thursday. Mommy and I were picking up Andrew at preschool. I had gotten my photographs back that morning.

"Yea!" he said. "Let's hurry home so I can see them!"

At home I showed him how I had pasted them into my crime notebook. "Here is a picture of Donald," I said. It was labeled: *Donald, our doorman. He says he did not see anything.*

The next picture was of Mrs. Farthing and

her tiny dog, Phyllis. I had taken their picture while Mrs. Farthing was checking her mail. She and Phyllis both looked surprised. Underneath the picture I had written: *Mrs. Farthing. Was she really at the vet's with Phyllis?*

Andrew and I looked at all the pictures carefully. Andrew was very excited when I showed him my photos of the police cars parked in front of our building.

"There are other cars here," he said, pointing. "Maybe one of them is the thief's."

"Maybe," I said. "There is Fred's delivery truck also. Maybe the thief was hiding in it when Fred drove away. But Fred said he did not see anybody. And here is a picture of Matt Dilley." I had told Andrew about finding Matt hiding in the dark in the basement. We both thought that was definitely fishy. What had he been doing? Waiting for an accomplice? Could Matt be part of a burglary ring?

I was not sure. I needed to gather more evidence before I made any accusations.

One thing was for sure: I was going to watch Matt like a hawk.

It is not so easy to watch someone like a hawk in a big city like Chicago. I could watch Matt only as long as he was in our building. As soon as he left the building with his mother or grandmother, I could not follow him.

It was driving me crazy.

For one thing, I was more and more sure that Matt had been in on the robbery. He was acting gigundoly sly. Every time I searched the building, I saw Matt. He was usually hiding under a table or behind a plant or beneath the stairs. If that does not sound like criminal behavior, what does?

But why would Matt steal paintings from his own grandmother? I could not figure it out. Unless someone else had put Matt up to it. Hmm. I needed more information.

I was close to blowing the case wide open — I could feel it. Matt was the key to the whole thing.

On Friday morning, Mommy sent me down to the lobby to check our mail. I was heading back toward the elevator with it when I spotted the tips of some scuffed red sneakers poking out from behind the curtains in the lobby. Holding my breath, I snuck closer, closer. I peeked around the curtain.

Of course it was Matt. He was wearing his trenchcoat again. He had pulled the collar up to cover half of his face. He was hunched over, fumbling with something. What was it? I was so excited I almost squeaked.

Was this the clue I had been waiting for? Would this solve the mystery of the missing paintings? Very, very quietly, I inched closer. What was Matt doing? I could not see. Then all of a sudden, something shiny dropped out of his hand and clattered onto the marble floor of the lobby. I leaped over, snatched it up, and raced for the elevator before Matt even knew what had happened.

"Hey!" he yelled. "Wait! Come back here!"

But I flashed through the elevator doors and pounded the DOOR CLOSE button. The last thing I saw was Matt's angry face as the doors closed between us.

I did not think Matt could run up five flights of stairs as fast as the elevator could go. But I still looked both ways when the doors opened on my floor. My heart pounding, I raced for our doorway and fumbled with my key. I thought I heard Matt running up the stairs! Finally I burst into the apartment, pushed Rocky out of the way with my foot, and slammed the door shut.

"Karen? Please do not slam the door, honey," called Mommy from the other room.

"Okay," I called back.

Only then did I look down to see the valuable clue that I held in my hand. I gasped. It was an audiocassette.

I Was All Wrong

An audiocassette! For just a moment I stared at it. Then, feeling only a tiny bit guilty, I ran into Andrew's room. I popped the tape into his My First Tape Player. I knew it was wrong for me to listen to a tape that was not mine. But it was a very huge clue. It was evidence. That made it a little less wrong, in my opinion.

Eagerly I rewound the tape. I pictured myself taking the tape to the police department. I saw all the police officers looking shocked and impressed that I had solved the mystery. Poor Matt. He would probably be led away in chains. I wondered how many years a seven-year-old would serve in jail for stealing.

And I had the evidence right here. This tape probably would tell me the names of other burglars he knows, lists of places that sell stolen things . . . and the hiding place of the paintings.

I pressed the play button.

". . . Wednesday afternoon, two o'clock," whispered Matt's voice.

I felt a shiver run down my spine.

"I am here in the lobby," whispered Matt. "I see Mrs. Peterson picking up her mail. She is still one of my main suspects."

My eyebrows lifted. Suspects? Matt had suspects? What did this mean?

"She has been trying to buy Grandma's apartment for years," whispered Matt's tape. "Maybe she stole the paintings to scare Grandma away."

I put my hand over my mouth. Then there

was rustling and a clicking noise on the tape.

"Now it is Thursday morning," I heard Matt whisper. "That nosy Karen Brewer has been acting very suspicious. I see her lurking all over the building. Just the other morning she was in the basement, poking around. She *said* she was looking for her cat. A likely story. She probably planted the cat there to give herself an alibi."

I gasped.

"The question is, what is she hiding? Is she working with the thief?"

I leaned over and clicked off the tape. I had heard enough. This was incredible. The tape showed that Matt had been doing exactly what I was doing: detective work. He was trying to solve the mystery of the missing paintings. The only difference was that he had been taping his notes. I had been writing mine down. He had called me "that nosy Karen Brewer." The nerve! How dare he suspect me!

Just then the doorbell rang. I knew who it was.

"I will get it, Mommy!" I called.

I hesitated just a moment before I answered the door. This would be difficult. I would have to give Matt his tape back. Even worse, I would have to admit that I had been wrong about him. I hate admitting I am wrong.

My New Partner

I opened the door (after making sure Rocky was nowhere around). There he was: Matt Dilley.

In one hand he carried a tiny cassette player. Its microphone was clipped to his collar. He was tapping one red sneaker angrily.

Without saying a word, he held out his hand. I put the tape in it. Frowning at me, he started to walk away.

"Wait!" I blurted out. "I have to show you something!"

Matt paused. He turned. "What is it?"

"Can you come in for a minute?" I asked.

Matt's eyes narrowed suspiciously. "Just for a minute."

Inside, Matt sat on the living room couch. Midgie and Rocky inspected him, then went back to their naps.

I got something from my room. I handed it to Matt.

"Here," I said. "I heard your notes. It's only fair that you read mine."

Matt looked surprised as he flipped through my crime notebook. He read my list of suspects. He frowned when he read my notes about him, but there was nothing I could do about that.

"I was wrong about your being part of the burglary ring," I said. "But you were wrong about me too. Look, we are both working on the same case. It only makes sense that we start working together. If we put our notes together and use our heads, I am sure we will solve the mystery. With both of our sharp minds on the trail, that burglar does not stand a chance. What do you say?"

Matt pinched his lip between his thumb and index finger while he thought. Finally he nodded. "Okay. I see your point. If we do not join up, we will just get in each other's way. We might even tip off the burglar about what we are doing. So I guess we should be partners."

I smiled and held out my hand. "Hello, partner."

Matt shook my hand and smiled too.

Then we told each other everything we could think of about the burglary. We made a new list of suspects, including Mrs. Peterson, Donald, and Mrs. Lawrence. Mrs. Lawrence lived in the apartment next to ours. Mommy had mentioned that she collected paintings. Ha, I thought. Maybe she does not care where the paintings come from.

I started to feel very excited. It had been fun working on the mystery before, but now that I had a full-time partner, it was even better.

And guess what. Matt thought the paintings were hidden in the building too!

"If no one saw the burglar carrying out the paintings," he said, "then he must have hidden them somewhere."

"Right," I said. "But where? I have been searching and searching. There are not many places where you could hide a humongous painting in a frame."

"But that is just it!" cried Matt. "They are not humongous paintings in frames. They are really pretty small." He held up his hands to show me. The paintings were about the size of two pieces of construction paper taped together. "And the burglar cut them out of their frames," continued Matt. "So they could be rolled up, like a poster."

"Would that ruin the paintings?" I asked.

"No." Matt shook his head. "If the burglar was careful, they would still be okay. Hey! Would you like to see the scene of the crime? You can even see the picture frames."

My eyes grew big. "Yeah! That would be great!"

"Okay. Let's go to my grandmother's apartment," said Matt.

First I asked Mommy if I could go. She said yes, because she knew Matt's grandmother and knew where she lived.

So Matt and I ran downstairs to the fourth floor. Matt got out his key. I was gigundoly excited. I was about to see the scene of the crime.

The Scene of the Crime

Matt's grandmother's apartment was just like ours. The furniture was different, of course. But the hall was the same size, and the kitchen was in the same place, and the bedrooms and bathroom and living room and dining room were in the same places, with the same doors and windows and all.

But Mrs. Arthur (that's Matt's grandmother) had tons more stuff than Mommy and Seth and Andrew. That is because she had been living in her apartment for a long, long time. Paintings and pictures were hung all over the walls. There were big pieces of dark furniture. There were huge plants in huge pots. I felt as if I were in the middle of a furniture store.

"Look," said Matt. He turned on the light in the hallway. "This is where the paintings were."

On the wall I saw two empty picture frames, still hanging among a ton of other framed pictures. I looked at the frames carefully. They were gigundoly fancy, all carved and painted with gold, but they were pretty small.

"Hello," said a voice.

I turned and saw an elegant older woman. Her gray hair was fixed in a bun, and she was wearing a handsome purple suit.

"Hello," I said.

"Grandma," said Matt, "this is Karen Brewer. Karen, this is my grandma, Mrs. Arthur."

"Pleased to meet you," I said politely.

"How do you do," said Mrs. Arthur with

a smile. "Are you helping Matt with the case?"

Matt puffed up his chest proudly. I was glad that Mrs. Arthur was not teasing us about solving the crime. (You know how grown-ups can be sometimes.)

"Yes," I said. "I did not realize the stolen paintings were so small."

"That is what is unusual," said Mrs. Arthur. "The thief took two small paintings. It is true they are valuable, but this larger painting over here is actually worth quite a bit more." She pointed to a painting in a fancy frame. To tell you the truth, it looked like someone had just thrown some paint on a canvas. *I* could have painted a better picture.

"The other odd thing," said Mrs. Arthur, "is that both of these little paintings were given to me by an old suitor, a man I knew before I married Matt's grandfather. Here, I will show you a picture of him."

She opened a drawer and pulled out a framed photograph. It showed a nice-looking man with a mustache, wearing a top hat.

I frowned at the picture. "He looks familiar," I said. "I feel as if I have seen him before. Does he live in this building?"

"Oh, goodness no," laughed Mrs. Arthur. "Poor Howard — I have not heard from him in over thirty years. But he was an actor, and he appeared in one or two minor pictures, a long time ago. Perhaps you happened to see him in one."

"Perhaps," I said, but I did not think so. He did look familiar, though.

"Grandma was an actress too, but in plays, not movies," said Matt. "She was on Broadway a lot."

"Oh, that was a long time ago." Mrs. Arthur blushed and looked a little embarrassed. "I have not acted in a long, long time."

"That is too bad," I said.

"I think so too," said Matt. "I think Grandma should start acting again."

"No, those days are over for me," said

Mrs. Arthur. "I left the stage when I married my husband and had my family. I do not really miss it. I am happy taking care of my plants and doing my volunteer work."

Soon I had to go home for lunch. I said good-bye to Matt and Mrs. Arthur. Matt and I agreed to meet later in the afternoon to continue working on our case.

I thought about everything as I headed back upstairs to Mommy's apartment. The case was getting more complicated all the time.

A New Clue

"I wish I could come with you," said Andrew.

"I wish you could too," I said. I took another bite of my peanut butter sandwich. "I did not know you had a play date today."

It was later that afternoon. I had been waiting anxiously for Andrew to come home from preschool so I could tell him everything. While we ate lunch I told him about working with Matt — and that I had been wrong about him. I also told Andrew about Mrs. Arthur, who had once been a Broadway actress.

I was hoping that Andrew could join Matt and me this afternoon, when we started searching the building again. After all, three searchers are better than two. But Andrew was supposed to go to his friend Rachel's apartment to play. (She lived down the block.)

"Maybe I can help you tomorrow," said Andrew.

"Yeah," I said.

That afternoon Matt and I met in the lobby. We tried to act casual, as if we were just regular kids. We did not want to tip off any burglars who might be watching. As usual, the lobby was a busy place, with people coming and going. The Fed Ex man dropped off several packages. Mr. Lacey took his four pug dogs out for a walk. The mail had not arrived yet.

Matt and I rode the elevator to the sixth floor. We searched the hallway again, but found nothing. There was no place to hide even small, rolled-up paintings.

We searched the fifth floor. Nothing. The fourth floor. Nothing. I was beginning to feel gigundoly discouraged. After all, we had both searched before. This was a big waste of time.

I sat down on the steps and put my chin in my hands.

"We are missing something," I said.

Matt sat down next to me. "We need a fresh lead," he agreed.

"We need a big clue," I said. "What could it be? What are we not seeing?" Then I had an idea. "Hey! What if the burglar was one of the police officers? I saw a TV show once and someone escaped because he was pretending to be a firefighter. What if the burglar was disguised as a police officer and just left with the other police officers?"

"But how will we know?" asked Matt.

"I have pictures of them!" I said. "Come on! I have pictures of practically everybody and everything!"

A Familiar Face

When Matt had seen my crime notebook before, he had not seen all my pictures of the suspects, or the other pictures I had taken of the building.

"Hey, here is Grandma's front door," he said, looking at one of my photos.

"Yup," I said. "And here is one of the lobby doors. And the door to the basement. And the inside of the elevator."

Matt turned the pages, pinching his lip between his thumb and his forefinger. "Gee, I recognize all these people," he said. "What did you do, hide by the mailboxes and spring out when they were picking up their mail?"

"Yes," I said. "That is why they look kind of surprised. And here, this picture is of all the police cars parked in the street below. I took it from our living room window. You can see some of the police officers."

Matt squinted at the picture. "They are much too tiny, though. I can't see their faces," he said, disappointed. "It was a good idea, but the police look like little blue grains of rice in this picture."

I was disappointed too. I looked at the picture again. In it were the two police cars, parked next to a brown car, a pale blue minivan, and Fred's delivery truck.

"Did you interview Fred Patterson, the delivery guy?" I asked.

Matt nodded. "He was here that day but did not see anything."

"That is what he told me, too," I said. "He is a nice guy."

"Yeah."

I thought for awhile longer. Something was bothering me, but I did not know what it was. I thought and thought. Slowly I turned the pages of my crime notebook. I looked at the pictures. Here was a shot of our mail carrier. Here was a photo of the delivery boy from the grocery store. I stared at him, but he did not look suspicious. Here was a shot of Donald the doorman talking to Fred Patterson.

I looked at Donald. It was just same old Donald. Then I looked at Fred. It was same old Fred, but there was also something else about him.

"You know, Fred looks familiar to me," I said.

Matt snorted. "Of course he does. You see him practically every day."

"No, I mean, I feel like I have seen him somewhere else. Maybe on TV or something. Hey! Maybe on *Crimewatchers*!"

Crimewatchers is one of my favorite TV shows. It has stories about real criminals and how their crimes were solved. Maybe one day I would be on *Crimewatchers* myself, as a crime-solver.

Matt rolled his eyes. "I do not think so, Karen," he said.

"Okay, maybe not on *Crimewatchers*," I said. "But I still think I have seen Fred somewhere else."

"Whatever," said Matt.

We put my book away and went back down to the lobby, because we could not think of anything else to do. We sat on the steps leading up to the second floor, watching people. I just love watching people. People are interesting, even if they are not crime suspects.

Our mail carrier came and went. Somebody dropped off a bouquet of flowers. A boy dropped off some dry cleaning for apartment twenty-four.

"Hi, Donald!" said Fred Patterson. He gave Donald a smile and winked at us kids. We smiled and waved at him. Then Donald signed for a package for Mr. Winkle in apartment thirty-nine. "I also have a pickup from Mrs. Posden on the fifth floor," said Fred.

"Okeydoke," said Donald.

Fred got into the elevator. Silently Matt and I watched the numbers light up as the elevator rose. One, two, three, four. Number four lit up, and we waited for five. But five stayed dark.

I frowned.

Matt frowned. "I thought Fred was getting off on five," he said.

Then I gasped. "Oh, my gosh! I know where I have seen Fred before!"

The Suspect Trapped

"Where?" Matt asked.

Suddenly I felt confused. I was sure about something, but it did not make sense. "Fred is the man in that photograph in your grandmother's apartment," I said slowly. "The man who gave her the paintings, before she married your grandfather."

Matt stared at me. "That is impossible!" he said. "Fred is much too young. That picture was taken a very long time ago."

"I know," I said, shaking my head. "It

does not make sense. But I am sure that Fred is the man in the picture. Somehow."

"Anyway, he sure is acting fishy," said Matt. "Come on. Let's see why Fred got off on the fourth floor."

We started to run up the stairs. (Taking the elevator would give us away.) We were rounding the corner to the third floor when we heard footsteps on their way down. Matt and I scrambled to one side and hid by the trash chute. We saw Fred, slinking quietly downstairs!

"Where is he going?" I whispered.

"Maybe to the basement," whispered Matt.

"Let's go tell your grandmother," I said. "She will know what to do."

We ran up the stairs to the fourth floor. (My legs were very tired.) We told Mrs. Arthur that Fred was acting suspicious. I said I thought he was definitely the man in her photograph, her old suitor. Mrs. Arthur frowned. She did not know what to think. But she called Donald. He said he would meet us in the basement.

Luckily the elevator was still right there on the fourth floor. The doors whooshed open and Matt, Mrs. Arthur, and I piled in. I pressed B, for the basement.

Down in the basement, we stood for a moment, not knowing which direction to head. Donald came down the stairs from the lobby. We looked up and down the hallway. We did not see anyone. It was very quiet. To tell you the truth, it was a little bit creepy.

"Now, why are we looking for Fred down here?" asked Donald.

Matt and I looked at each other. If we were right, it would be great. If we were wrong, a lot of grown-ups would be upset.

"Um," I said. "We were just wondering about —"

"They think he took my paintings," said Mrs. Arthur firmly. "And I for one want to find out if that is true."

We looked all over and did not find Fred anywhere. Donald knew he had not left through the lobby, so where could he be? He had not gone upstairs on the elevator because *we* had been on the elevator. It was very mysterious.

We were in the brightly lit laundry room, wondering what to do next. Then Donald's eyes narrowed. He pointed at a closet door that was in one corner of the laundry room. As quietly as possible, the four of us tiptoed to it.

I put my hand over my mouth. We could hear faint noises coming from inside! I was about to burst with excitement.

Donald squared his shoulders. Then he lunged forward, grabbed the doorknob, and yanked the door open.

There was Fred, holding several mailing tubes!

The Criminal Is Caught

I do not think I have ever seen anyone look as surprised as Fred looked when Donald yanked the door open on him. His eyes were wide, and his mouth formed a large "O."

"The jig is up!" I cried.

"My goodness!" said Fred with a little laugh. He put his cap back on his head and pushed the mailing tubes into a large canvas pouch. "What is this?"

"Well, Fred," said Donald. "That is what we want to know. Why are you down here in the basement? I thought you were picking up a package on the fifth floor."

Fred tried to smile. "Um, well, Mrs. Posden said, um, she had, uh, stored the packages down here. . . ."

Donald frowned at him and crossed his arms. Matt and I stood back. I did not know what to think. Fred was a nice guy. He had always been so friendly.

"What is in those mailing tubes, Fred?" asked Mrs. Arthur in a no-nonsense tone.

"Huh? Oh, these." Fred looked as if he were trying to think. He started to edge out of the closet. He looked up at us again. "How would I know? They belong to Mrs. Posden."

Donald tried to pick up one of the cardboard tubes. "As the doorman, I am responsible for everything that goes in and out of this building," he said.

But Fred pulled away from Donald. "They are not yours," he said loudly. Then he pushed Donald out of the way and ran for the door.

"Do not let him get away!" I cried.

Donald shoved a laundry cart toward Fred. It bumped his legs and he stumbled. But he caught his balance and rushed through the laundry room doorway. We raced after him, but then we heard a big crash and a muffled "Oof!"

In the hallway, Fred had run into Mrs. Borgen from apartment twenty-six. She had been carrying a humongous pile of laundry, and now it was all over everything. Fred and Mrs. Borgen were sitting on the ground. Fred picked himself up fast and tried to run down the hall, but he slipped on Mrs. Borgen's comforter cover and fell again.

"Just a minute, young man!" commanded Mrs. Arthur. She held up her hand, and Fred looked at her. "You just stop right there. The police are already on their way. In fact, I believe I hear them coming down the stairs now."

We all listened, but I could not hear anything.

"There is no point in resisting," continued

Mrs. Arthur firmly. "It is time to tell us the truth."

Fred looked confused and panicky, but he stayed put. He looked toward the stairs to see if the police were coming.

"That is better," said Mrs. Arthur. "Now, let's get to the bottom of this. Is Patterson your real name?"

"Why do you want to know?" asked Fred grumpily.

"Because I think your last name is Morris," said Mrs. Arthur. Her face softened. "You are the spitting image of Howard Morris, who was a very dear friend of mine a long time ago."

When Fred heard this, he sort of crumpled down onto the pile of laundry again. Mrs. Borgen stared up at Mrs. Arthur, then at Fred, then at Mrs. Arthur again. Donald leaned over and helped her up. Then he made sure she was okay.

"I am going to the lobby to sit down for a moment," said Mrs. Borgen. "I will get my laundry later." She left.

I turned to Fred. "Is it true?" I asked. "Are you related to Howard Morris?"

Fred nodded and rubbed his hands over his face. "Yes," he said. "Howard Morris was my father. My brother and I changed our name after Dad died."

Matt and I stared at each other, and I nodded. I knew it!

The Paintings Are Found

For a moment no one said anything. Then Mrs. Arthur stepped forward and gently took the mailing tubes out of Fred's canvas bag. He did not try to stop her. Mrs. Arthur opened the ends of the tubes and looked inside. She looked at Matt and me and nodded. From one of the tubes she pulled a small piece of stiff, rolled canvas. She opened it up and showed us what looked like a fuzzy landscape. It was small, and very pretty. But I could not believe that it was worth tons of money.

"So it was you, after all," said Donald to Fred. Fred looked ashamed. He nodded.

"The paintings are not damaged," said Mrs. Arthur. "Fortunately. But tell me, why did you do it? You have been delivering packages here for years."

Fred sighed. "Well, it is a long story."

"Please tell us," I said. "We want to know."

Fred nodded. "After my father knew you, he married my mother," he said. "He quit acting, and started his own company. The company did very well, and he and my mother were very happy together. They had my younger brother and me. Then my mother died. My father became so sad that he could not work anymore. My brother and I were too young to know what to do. My father lost all his money, and the company went out of business. Last year my father died also. That's when I changed my name — so that bill collectors would not bother me."

"Oh, no," said Mrs. Arthur softly. "I had no idea."

"That is a terrible story," said Matt. I nodded.

"Not long after my father died, I was going through his things, dividing them between my brother and me," said Fred. "I found a note that mentioned the paintings. He did not say who he had given them to. Those paintings would have meant so much to us! My younger brother is in medical school. But we have no money for him to finish his education. He might never be a doctor. Then one day, when I was delivering a package to you, I saw the paintings on your wall! I was amazed. I felt that I needed them more than you did, and that my father should have given them to my brother and me, instead of to you."

Fred hung his head. I felt like crying. Mrs. Arthur looked very, very sad also.

"I do not know what I was thinking," said Fred. "I have never taken anything in my life. But I stole the paintings one day while you were out. I am ashamed of what I did. I know my father would be very unhappy if he were alive."

Fred looked at us. "Anyway, I am glad it is over. Once I had the paintings, I did not know what to do with them. That is why I hid them in the building. They are too famous to sell, and I do not even know anyone who would buy stolen paintings. Today I wanted to look at them again. I was trying to figure out if I could sneak them back into your apartment somehow. I was very stupid. I am glad you have them back."

Just then the police finally did come running down the stairs.

And That Wraps It Up

The two police officers hurried down the hall and looked at us. They saw Donald, Matt, Mrs. Arthur, and me all standing around poor Fred, who was still sitting on the laundry.

"Um, a Mrs. Borgen called us?" said one of the police officers. "Is there a problem here?"

"Yes," said Fred, standing up. "You must arrest me for burglary." He told them how he had stolen Mrs. Arthur's paintings.

"So, it was an inside job," said the other

officer. "I thought so. Mrs. Arthur, we will need you to come down to the station to press charges against him."

Mrs. Arthur threw her head back. "I cannot!" she said dramatically. "This poor man is not a criminal. He is just down on his luck. I think we should let him go."

Matt and I stared at each other. This was the most exciting day I had had all summer.

"Um, well, we cannot just let him go," explained the officer. "He has confessed to breaking the law. But your leniency will make things easier for him, if he has no criminal record."

"I am guilty," said Fred. "I know I must pay for what I did."

But before the police took him away, Mrs. Arthur went up to her apartment. She came back with the lovely framed photograph of Howard Morris, Fred's father.

"I want you to have this," said Mrs. Arthur. "Howard was a wonderful person, and you were lucky to have him as your father. I promise to stay in touch with you, and help you in any way I can."

"Thank you," said Fred. "You have been very kind."

We all watched sadly as Fred climbed into the police car. Matt and I had solved the mystery. I felt both glad and sad.

Several days later, I heard that Fred would not go to prison. Instead, the police would just keep an eye on him for awhile. I was very glad.

Mommy and Seth and Andrew could not believe that Matt and I had solved such a big mystery. They were very proud, and they were glad we had gotten Mrs. Arthur and Donald to help us, instead of chasing Fred all by ourselves.

With the mystery solved, I had a lot more time to play. Matt started hanging out with Andrew and me. We went to the little corner park together. Sometimes we walked Midgie around the block.

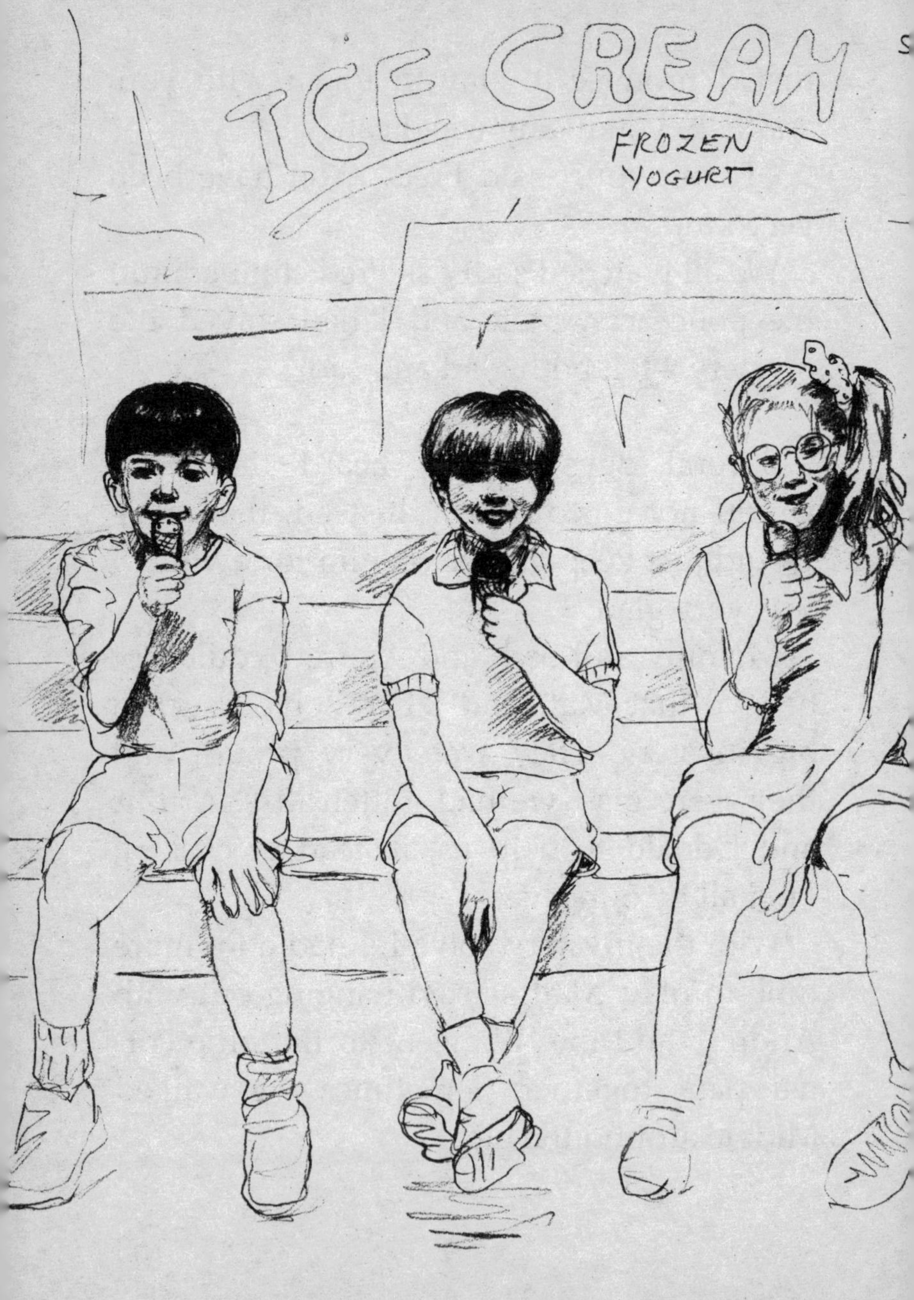
ICE CREAM
FROZEN
YOGURT

One day Mommy took us to get ice-cream cones at the ice-cream parlor three blocks away.

"Maybe one day we should open our own detective agency," said Matt, licking his cone.

"We could call it K and M, Private Eyes," I said.

"Or K and M and A, Private Eyes," said Andrew. "Next time I will skip preschool for a couple of days."

I laughed. "Good idea."

"Oh, guess what," said Matt. A drop of chocolate ice cream splashed onto his red sneaker. "Grandma says she might try acting again. She always said she would not, but after catching Fred, she thinks she might try it after all."

"You mean she liked pretending the police were on the way?" I asked.

"Yup," said Matt. "And she did a good job. We did not know that Mrs. Borgen had gone upstairs to call the police. But Grandma enjoyed acting as if she knew they were already coming. So she is going to try out for a play."

"That is wonderful!" I said. "I will come back to Chicago for her opening night, no matter what."

"Good," said Matt.

The three of us (and Mommy) walked back to Mommy's apartment. I still did not want to live in Chicago. But I was having a great visit. And Mommy, Seth, and Andrew would be coming back to Stoneybrook in a few months. Hmm, I thought. Maybe Matt should come to Stoneybrook too. Then we could solve an exciting Stoneybrook mystery!

L. GODWIN

About the Author

ANN M. MARTIN lives in New York City and loves animals, especially cats. She has two cats of her own, Gussie and Woody.

Other books by Ann M. Martin that you might enjoy are *Stage Fright*; *Me and Katie (the Pest)*; and the books in *The Baby-sitters Club* series.

Ann likes ice cream and *I Love Lucy*. And she has her own little sister, whose name is Jane.

Little Sister

Don't miss #100

KAREN'S BOOK

Hmm. Maybe I could write the story of *my* life the way Laura Ingalls Wilder wrote the story of hers. Only I would illustrate my story too. The whole book would be about me, Karen Brewer. And my family and friends because they are part of my life too. Ooh! This was a gigundoly good idea.

Where would I start? I decided to start with the day I was born. That was a long time ago. Seven years. I did not remember much. In fact, I did not remember anything about the day I was born. Mommy and Daddy had told me stories, though. And I knew Daddy had pictures. I needed to do some research.